Habititus Fever:
Infected With a Desire to Help Others

Habititus Fever
Infected With a Desire to Help Others
By Wanda Jones-Nelson and Ron Kelso

Illustrations by Jack Foster and Caleb Davis
Interior Layout & Design by T.L. Price Freelance

ISBN 978-0-9914127-0-9

Email us at: Habititus@FoxValleyHabitat.org

Habititus is a pending trademark of
Fox Valley Habitat for Humanity.

Habititus Fever

Infected With a Desire To Help Others

By Wanda Jones-Nelson and Ron Kelso
with Discussion Questions

Illustrations by Jack Foster and Caleb Davis

Other Books by Wanda Jones-Nelson

Adventure on the Tyler City Trail
Available through
www.tatepublishing.com/bookstore
Or wherever books are sold

In Loving Memory of Kevin Kelso

It was Kevin's vision to bring the youth he was working with in the church youth group and for his dad to bring the adults to volunteer at a Habitat for Humanity build-site. Kevin loved helping others who were struggling and he saw the importance of helping a deserving family build their Habitat for Humanity home. While Kevin lost his battle with depression as a teenager, his legacy lives on.

Since Habitat for Humanity's motivation is Christian-based, it is only natural for churches to partner with them to help families earning lower-wages into home-ownership. Community Christian Church in Naperville, IL stepped up and helped the Kelso family do a dinner-auction to raise enough money to sponsor a home with Habitat for Humanity. Kevin's father continues to volunteer nearly every day to transform deserving families' lives through Fox Valley Habitat for Humanity in Montgomery, IL. Posthumously, the youth did work on the home by doing all the landscaping while the adults helped with the construction of the home.

We are thankful to have had Kevin as our son and look forward to the time when we will all be reunited in heaven.

With all our love,

Dad and Mom

"Mercy to the needy is a loan to God, and God pays back those loans in full"
(Proverbs 19:7)

TABLE OF CONTENTS

ACKNOWLEDGMENTS

I would like to express my deepest appreciation to Mrs. Wanda Jones-Nelson for using her gift of writing to create this story that has been on my heart. It started with a goal to empower students to learn that they can make a huge difference in the lives of others. What a blessing it is that this God loving woman wrote this story to benefit Habitat for Humanity. Without Wanda this story would never have been completed. By including real life challenges, her gift of writing makes our story come alive and have lasting value. As a retired teacher and parent, I know the opportunity parents, grandparents, teachers, and church leaders will have to discuss many real life situations in a way that is appropriate for each child's age. It is because of her thought provoking style that the discussion questions can help children to learn and grow from this book.

Thank you Wanda for all you do to help others. What you have accomplished in writing this book is to provide a tool for adults to help their children or students understand that they can make a difference even if they act alone. And if they get others involved, they can start something as contagious as Habititus Fever.

~Ron Kelso

I would like to thank Mr. Ron Kelso, the Executive Coordinator of Fox Valley Habitat for Humanity, for working with me to write this children's book for Habitat. It is an honor to be a part of this venture to benefit Habitat for Humanity and to work with this wonderful man of God who has such a caring heart for people. I pray that this book will inspire future generations to continue the legacy that Millard Fuller began and that you too, will catch Habititus Fever. I also want to express my appreciation to Mr. Kelso for writing the discussion questions, and for all of his help in story editing, story suggestions, and tirelessly answering my questions as I learned about this amazing ministry, Habitat for Humanity.

In addition, it was Ron's creative ability that invented the title, "Habititus Fever," that was the basis of this story. I especially want to praise God for His hand on this book and the miraculous way He has worked out every detail far better than we could have done ourselves.

~Wanda Jones-Nelson

ENDORSEMENTS

"When our family started reading Habititus Fever, we expected this to be a positive, happy ending type of book. The cover picture was cute and it was about a great organization that we have the honor to be part of – Habitat for Humanity. But...as we read each chapter, it always ended in a big question mark! It kept us guessing, reading, and trying to figure out how all of this would come together. Along the way, we met many very interesting and realistic characters – most of whom were full of energy with good morals and a can-do attitude. This is a book that deals with some tough issues and moves very gracefully through to resolve them. Most of all, it shows how a community or any group of people can help a family who is "just barely making it" due to the high cost of rent and the near impossibility of financing a house.

Everyday community members can make a difference by donating their time in sweat equity, knowledge, building supplies, food for the volunteers and many other resources. These same people are making families' dreams come true. We are proud recipients of such generous acts and we are forever grateful. It has changed our lives and our outlook. I am excited to find out what kind of differences and blessings my children and I will be contributing to this world due to the inspiration and secure foundation Habitat for Humanity has given us."

~The Fortuny-Walker family.

"Habitat for Humanity is a visionary way to assist people in obtaining affordable housing based on the very Biblical concept of helping a neighbor and creating independence rather than dependence. Because recipients of housing are required to pay a zero percent mortgage on the cost of construction and to put in 'sweat equity' helping build other Habitat homes as well as their own, Habitat doesn't add to a dependency culture, but a responsibility culture. My wife was on the Habitat International Board for a number of years and remains active in the organization. She has traveled to most of the 50 states and numerous countries across the globe helping to build houses with Habitat. Ron Kelso and Wanda Jones-Nelson capture the essence of the Habitat experience in their book that will encourage, inspire, and teach how Christians can do more than hope for better housing for their neighbors, but help build it. I hope you will be blessed!"

~Governor Mike Huckabee

"What a wonderful way to illustrate and introduce the story of Habitat for Humanity through the eyes and experiences of children. This book touches the human spirit on complex social issues like... homelessness, bullying, anger and family. You have a gifted way of bringing to light in clear, practical and simple ways complex issues facing our world today. A must read!"

~George Vera, Treasurer of

Christian Motorcyclists Association (CMA)

Aurora, IL Chapter (Chariots for Christ)

"A wonderful story erasing common stereotypes that accompany the homeless; providing a glimpse into the pressure, fear, confusion, and insecurity that many homeless feel; and creating in each of us a deeper sensitivity, motivation and challenge to reach out to those in need. 'Habititus Fever'—may we all come down with a serious case of it and joyfully spread it to all with whom we have contact."

~Scott Poling, Senior Pastor

Harvest New Beginnings in Oswego, Illinois

"Wanda has a way of reaching the hearts of children through her writings. She brought together the military and their families at home and how God wants us to take care of those in need at a level that children can understand. This is an excellent book to encourage children and their families to reach out and give and not to think selfishly. Once again, I am amazed at how she puts things into prospective that should be carried on through generations to come."

~Mrs. Pam Hapner, 3rd and 4th grade teacher

Covenant Christian School, Aurora, IL

CHAPTER 1
The Project

The April rain fell mercilessly as Victoria Dodson pulled a brown blanket tightly over herself and her ten-year old daughter Brittany. Brittany's curly red pigtails, which had been so carefully adorned with blue ribbons earlier, were falling out of place. Victoria was thankful that they at least had the shelter of the bridge overhead. Suddenly, lightening cracked and hit the garbage can that sat near the end of the bridge. Sparks flew into the rolling river.

Brittany screamed. Tears streamed down her face almost as fast as the rushing river flowed alongside them. "Mom, why do we have to sleep in the park? I want to go home."

"I know dear, but we can't do that right now." She snuggled up close to her daughter.

"I don't understand, mom." Brittany buried her head under the blanket as another bolt of lightning struck near the dam. The storm raged on through the night. The river's waves crashed against the banks where Victoria and her daughter tried to sleep. They had never been homeless before. Evicted from their apartment, Victoria's dream of owning her own home seemed to have drifted away like the debris that floated down the river. She didn't understand how this could happen to them. She was always a hard worker, though she never made much money. She was very responsible with her money but never expected to lose her job.

o o o

Alexandria, Brianna, and Caitlin met on the playground of Smith School on Aurora's West Side, twenty minutes before school started. They liked to come early so they could visit and play before class started. The girls were in the fifth grade and had been together since kindergarten.

"The bus should be here soon," Ten-year-old Alexandria said, as she put her backpack down and ran for a swing.

"I wonder if DeVontay and Maddison will be here today?" Brianna ran to get the swing next to "Alex" as she called her.

"Why shouldn't they be here?" Caitlin asked, jumping onto the swing next to Brianna.

"I heard their little brother has the chicken pox. Usually all the kids in a family gets it if one has it, don't they?" Brianna swung higher into the air.

"Sometimes, but not always," Alex answered, suddenly stopping her swing. "Look at that huge puddle! Boy, it really rained hard last night. Did you hear all that thunder?" She ran to the puddle and made a boat out of a candy wrapper that had a couple of ants crawling on it. "Hey, come and look at the ants—they're going sailing." Alex giggled and watched as the candy-wrapper ship and ants floated from one side of the puddle to the other.

"I didn't hear anything. When I snuggle down into my comforter and pillow, I don't hear a sound. I love my bed and my room," Brianna said as she jumped out of her swing and joined Alex at the giant puddle.

"Hey, look, here comes the bus. I hope DeVontay and Maddy are on it—school isn't as fun when they are not here," Caitlin shouted, as she pulled out the handle on her backpack, rolling it by the wheels so she didn't have to carry it.

"Look, there they are." Alex pointed to DeVontay and Maddison. Though they were fraternal twins, they still very much resembled each other. She waved frantically until they spotted her.

"Hi, you guys, what's up?" Maddison smiled, adjusting her backpack.

"Oh, we were just wondering if you'd be here today since Micah has the chicken pox. We thought that maybe you two would have it by now too." Brianna smoothed down her wavy brown hair, which bounced from under her pink hat—she loved hats and was rarely seen without one.

"No such luck. It would be great to have a vacation from school, but I don't look so good in polka dots." DeVontay polked at his face, making little dots with his finger. They all laughed.

"What's so funny?" Nehemiah asked as he snuck up behind Brianna and covered her eyes with his hands.

"Quit that. You scared me, you goofball." Brianna softly elbowed him in the stomach then giggled.

"Ouch!" Nehemiah hunched over, pretending to be in pain.

"Micah is almost over them now. He's not contagious anymore. It looks like we're not going to catch them this time. Tomorrow, mom's even going to let him go back to school." DeVontay dropped the apple he was nibbling on. "Well, there goes the rest of my breakfast."

"I think it's about time to line-up. I'll beat you all to the front of the line." Maddison took off running toward the school door.

"What's your hurry?" Caitlin asked, running to catch up to her.

"I don't know. I just like to be first." Maddison grabbed her hat as it almost whisked onto the ground.

Assistant principal Wilson stepped outside and stood at the top of the stairs. She looked over all the children, and everyone knew that it was time to line-up. When the bell rang, everyone followed Maddison and lined-up behind her. Her purple, straw hat with a big white daisy perfectly accented her new purple-print crinkle top and white Capri jeans. She was a picture of perfection from her silky, black bob to her daisy-donned black flip-flops to accompany her hat. She and Brianna seemed to have a daily competition with their hats and accessories.

In fact, today, as they stood side-by-side in line, the girls saw they had dressed exactly alike, except for the color—Brianna loved pink and Maddison loved purple. All their friends burst out in laughter. Brianna and Maddison looked at each other—they exchanged scowls—then shared a hug.

"You sure have good taste, Brianna." Maddison giggled, pointing at Brianna.

"So do you. Great minds think alike, don't they?" Brianna rested her head on Maddison's then followed Miss Wilson into the school building. Caitlin, Nehemiah, Alex, and DeVontay followed them.

Their teacher, Mr. Navarro, was writing on the chalkboard as they walked into the classroom and took their seats. Nehemiah sat next to DeVontay in the back row; Alex and Caitlin sat in front of them; Brianna and Maddison sat in the lead desks. To them, it seemed they had been sitting that way since first grade. Right as the tardy bell rang, Brittany Dodson ran through the door, jumping in her seat next to Caitlin. Mr. Navarro looked at her and smiled. "It doesn't get much closer than that, does it?"

Brittany looked relieved and unzipped her bag and pulled out a few books. Her hair was still a little damp. She hoped everyone would just think it was wet from taking a shower. No one could know she was actually homeless and had slept outside during the storm. How could this have happened to them? If only her father were here. She missed him terribly.

"Alright, class, I hope you all had a nice evening last night. Let's try to get our thoughts on school work now." Mr. Navarro sat on top of his wooden desk, holding a piece of chalk in his hand. "I want to divide the class into four groups because I have a special project that I'd like to introduce to you. This is *very* important and will count as half of your grade

in social studies this quarter. So, first let's divide into our groups. I am going to divide the room into four parts. The dividing line will be right here in the middle, between you, DeVontay, and you, Billy. That will divide the class in half from side to side. Then, between you, Hayden, and also Brittany—front to back. Okay, look at your group. You will be spending a lot of time together in the next couple of weeks at school and out of school. Your assignment is simple: in our society right now, there are a lot of people who are hurting. There are a lot of reasons people are having a hard time, and a lot of ways people can get help. I want each group to think about that fact. Think of a situation, research ways that people might have gotten into it, then research organizations that are available to help them out. Be creative; go find someone to help. For now, I will give you the next thirty minutes to get together with your group and brainstorm. Go ahead and move your desks into a circle with your group, and get to work."

Alex's group was thrilled that they were going to be able to work together on this project. They didn't know Brittany too well, but working with her would help them all get better acquainted.

"Well, where should we begin?" DeVontay scratched his head with his pencil. It almost got stuck in his jet-black corn-rolled hair. He smiled, hoping that no one noticed.

"You are so funny." Caitlin giggled, as she got her desk turned. "I saw that."

"So, have you got any bright ideas?" DeVontay ignored her and tried to organize their team.

"A haircut?" She lowered it to a snicker.

"Okay, let's get down to some serious brainstorming." Mr. Navarro tried to appear annoyed by the noise, but he wasn't really. He was a special teacher—a rare find, some kids thought. He truly cared about his students, and they could tell. His wife was a teacher as well and they had a six-year-old daughter. Most of the girls thought he was dreamy with his jet-black shaggy hair, tan complexion, and dark brown eyes. There was a mutual respect between Mr. Navarro and the boys, as he listened when they talked.

"Remember what I said? This project is going to count as half of your grade this quarter." He sat down at his desk and watched as the class' four groups began to get organized. "Oh, by the way, I forgot to mention that the group that has the best project is going to be my guests at a Chicago Cubs home game!"

The whole classroom let out an excited cheer but then got down to serious project planning. Billy Todd, the meanest boy in the class, noticed Brittany's wet hair.

"What's the matter with your head, geek? Your hair dryer break down?" He laughed and pointed at Brittany. "You look like you slept in your clothes too. What a mess!"

"That will be enough out of you, Mr. Todd." Mr. Navarro scowled at Billy and gave Billy a displeased look.

"Yes, sir." Billy gave Brittany a "You better keep out of my way" scowl but then turned his attention to his group.

"What's up with him?" Nehemiah asked.

Brittany shrugged her shoulders then laid her head down on her desk, as she tried to hold back the tears.

"Don't worry about him, Brittany; he's nothing but a big bully. Just ignore anything that he says," Nehemiah said and patted her on the back.

Brittany tried to smile but couldn't.

"Excuse me," DeVontay said, trying to get everyone to focus on the project. "Who's got some ideas?" he added, looking around the circle of desks.

"Well," Nehemiah said, "I think that maybe we should elect someone to be in charge of our group and then decide when and where we are going to meet outside of class." He grabbed his notebook as he spoke. "I think that it would be fun to take turns meeting at all of our houses. All in favor, raise your hand." Everyone except Brittany raised their hand. "That's okay, Brittany. If you change your mind, let us know."

"Let's meet at my house, after dinner tonight. We can check out some things on-line. By then, maybe we will have some ideas to get started." Maddison smiled. "How does 7:00 p.m. sound? If you have a cell phone, set your alarm to help you remember."

"Sounds good to me." Alex nodded her head.

"Sure, I'll be there," Caitlin said.

"I'll reschedule my piano lesson," Brianna added, making a note of the time.

Everyone, including Brittany, agreed. They moved their desks back, just as Mr. Navarro announced that class time for the project was over.

Billy Todd banged his desk into Brittany's as he moved back into position, pinching her fingers between their desks. "Oh, I'm *so* sorry, geek," he said sarcastically. "Did I hurt you?"

"No." Brittany shook her head, fighting the urge to cry.

"What are you—some kind of a crybaby?"

"Just leave her alone!" DeVontay came to her rescue and stood in front of Billy's desk. His stare suggested that Billy stop. Their confrontation was interrupted when Mr. Navarro saw what was going on.

"Class! Get out your social studies books and read chapter 11. On Monday, we'll discuss the questions at the end of the chapter." He glared at Billy. "I want to see you after class."

"Yes, sir," Billy grumbled.

o o o

The last hours of class seemed to drag on. Brittany had a hard time focusing on her studies. Her mother was meeting her after school. Brittany wasn't sure what was going to happen tonight or how she was going to get to Maddison's house. She looked blankly at the pages of her social studies book, unable to read a word. Seeing a picture of a soldier made Brittany think of her father. Would she ever see him again? His plane was shot down in Iraq—he had been missing for weeks. How she longed to see him. What would *he* say about his wife and daughter living on the streets?

B-u-z-z-z-z-z!!! The dismissal bell sounded, startling her from her thoughts. Brittany packed up her books and was the first person out the door. In seconds, the classroom was emptied of everyone except Billy Todd. He remained at his desk as his teacher requested.

"Billy, your behavior toward Brittany was inexcusable," Mr. Navarro scolded. "I don't want to see any more of that. Do you understand?"

"Yes, sir, Mr. Navarro. I just have a problem with cry babies." Billy scowled at his teacher.

"In this class, you will keep those feelings to yourself. You might try to find out why she cries so easily, instead of being mean to her. I will not tolerate bullying in *my* class. Do I make myself clear?"

"Yes, sir, Mr. Navarro, I think that you are right. I am going to try to find out why she's such a crybaby." He grabbed his backpack and hurried out the door.

Mr. Navarro shook his head. He could see trouble coming with Billy Todd.

CHAPTER 2
Meeting at Maddison's

"Okay, everyone, follow me this way to the kitchen, and we'll get to work." Maddison motioned her friends to follow her through the double French doors that led to a cozy wood-paneled kitchen. "We're all here except Brit—" The doorbell sounded, interrupting her sentence. "Maybe that's her." She smiled and ran to the front door. Brittany stood there, looking as if she had just run for miles.

"Hi, Maddison." Brittany shyly stepped into the living room. "Sorry I'm late."

"No, you're fine. We're just getting started, actually. Follow me; we're going to work at the kitchen table. We're so glad that you could come. How did you get here—I didn't see anyone drop you off?"

"My mom dropped me off; she was in a hurry to get to the store. That's why you didn't see her."

"Oh, I see, anyway, I think you already know everyone here—Nehemiah, Alex, Brianna, Caitlin, my brother, DeVontay, and of course, you know me, Maddison." She pointed to each person as she introduced them. "Well, everyone have a seat and let's get started."

"Nehemiah, I saw you taking a lot of notes when Mr. Navarro gave us the assignment." Alex took her bright orange notebook and pen out of her tote as she spoke. "Do you have some introductory ideas?"

"I hear my parents talking a lot about how hard a time everyone is having now. Gas and grocery prices are so high. I don't think that we are going to be able to go on vacation this summer, mostly because of the price of gas." Nehemiah continued writing in his black notebook. He liked the color black. In fact, he always dressed in black with the leather vest he wore when he visited his grandparents' Christian motorcyclists chapter meeting. He also liked to wear a biker's do-rag on his head when he wasn't at school.

"Those are good points, Nehemiah." DeVontay chewed on the eraser tip of his pencil. "I know my dad is worried that he might lose his job."

"I might have to quit my piano lessons if my mom doesn't find another job soon," Brianna added, munching on a cookie from the plate in the middle of the table. "She lost her job a month ago."

"Wow, I'm sorry to hear that, Brianna." Caitlin placed her writing utensils and blue notebook in front of her, ready to take notes. Her blonde bangs fell over her blue eyes, as she reached down into her navy blue tote—almost everything she owned had to accentuate her eyes.

"What do you think, Brittany?" Maddison opened her pink notebook and took the seat next to Brittany.

"Well, my parents are doing just fine right now. My mom has a really good job, and my dad was a car salesman but is also a pilot in the Air Force Reserves. He got called back into active duty so he's over in Iraq right now, but we expect him to come home anytime now," Brittany said, doodling on her paper, barely looking up.

"That's great," Nehemiah said. "Does he get to email you very much?"

"Oh, yeah, almost every night." She kept doodling.

Alex jumped in, "Does *anyone* have a good idea for our project?"

"Do you think we could do something for people who have lost their jobs?" Nehemiah said as he wrote in his notebook.

"That might be too hard," DeVontay added. "Let's think of something easier to do. Who can we help?"

"Let's find some homeless person and see what we can do to give them some help." Caitlin said taking a sip from her cup of hot chocolate.

"So we're all agreed then?" Maddison questioned. "How hard can it be to find a homeless person?"

"Since tomorrow is Saturday, why don't we get together and go searching for someone who's homeless?" Nehemiah looked eagerly around the table for a reply.

"Okay." Alex stood up. "Where should we meet? How about your house, Brittany? Where do you live?"

Brittany looked up from her doodles, horrified. "No!" she answered sharply. "I mean my mom won't be home tomorrow. I can't have anyone over when she's not home."

"Oh, alright. We understand, Brittany," Nehemiah assured her. "I know… Why don't we meet down by the community center and just walk around to see if we can find a homeless person."

"That sounds like a good idea to me," Brittany said, looking relieved. "Let's meet at noon at the community center."

"I want everyone to go on line and see what kind of help is available to help homeless people. We can compare notes when we meet again." Maddison seemed to be taking charge of the group. "I think that this is a perfect project for us."

"I call this meeting adjourned until tomorrow at noon at the community center," DeVontay said. He stood up, pounded his mom's meat tenderizer three times on the table, trying to be like an official using his mallet.

"Good night, everyone," Maddison and DeVontay announced, as all of their friends walked out the front door, heading toward their homes.

"Don't you think that Brittany acted kind of funny tonight?" Maddison asked DeVontay.

"More funny than usual?" he replied.

"Yeah, she really looked worried when we wanted to meet at her house."

"You're right; I wonder why."

"Well, I guess that she'll tell us when she's ready."

"I suppose so. I hope that she's okay. I'm going to my room; I have more homework to do."

"Okay, I'm going to use the computer and see what more I can find out about homeless people. Good night, DeVontay."

"Good night, sis. See you in the morning."

CHAPTER 3

A Light in the Darkness

Brittany raced through the dark streets of her friend's neighborhood, to the place where her mother was waiting.

"Here I am, Brittany." Victoria Dodson stepped out from the bushes, into the streetlight. "How was your meeting?"

"It went okay, mom. I just don't know how I am going to keep them from finding out that we got kicked out of our apartment. In fact, homeless people are what they decided to do for our project. They are meeting tomorrow to try to find someone to help—they are looking for someone like us!" Brittany hugged her mother. "I am so worried that they will find out about us."

"It will be okay. You'll see, sweetheart." They headed back towards the river where Victoria had their blankets hidden.

"Mom, have you heard from dad? I miss him so much." Brittany wiped a tear from her eye. "I need to know what's going on, mom. I'm old enough; I can handle anything after this. Please tell me what you know," Brittany said, as they neared their river camp.

"You're right, Brittany. I just didn't want to worry you more than I had to. I know this is hard on you, but it will get better soon. I'm sure it will. We'll talk when we get back to our blankets."

"Mom, I don't like it down by the river. It scares me."

"Don't worry, Brittany, I'm going to try to get us into a church's PADS program for tomorrow night. We can do this for just one more night, can't we? Be a brave soldier, like daddy. Just know that I won't let anything happen to you, sweetheart. Please believe me. I applied for a couple of jobs today too, and I still have my cell phone. We'll be okay. Here are our blankets, right in the bushes where I hid them. See, they stayed soft and dry in this plastic bag. So help me spread them over here, under the bridge, and we'll be nice and cozy. It's warm tonight; and I bought this flashlight. Look, let me help you do your homework. I'll hold the flashlight for you. Do what you can tonight, and we'll go to the library tomorrow. You can finish your work there."

"Oh mom, I don't want to go to any church around here. Someone at school will find out. I'd just die of embarrassment, really. Please don't. I'd rather stay here! As long as I know it won't be for long, right? I promise I won't be scared anymore. Please just hold the flashlight, mom. I have a lot of math homework tonight. I finished everything else in study hall. My social studies project is the most important thing we are working on. We are going to research organizations that help homeless people. We are meeting tomorrow at the community center at noon." Brittany opened her math book and worked on her assignment, as her mother shined the flashlight on her paper.

"I wish I could help you with that, Honey, but the math you do seems so different from the way we did it—I'm kind of lost. At least I know how to hold a flashlight." Brittany's mom smiled, secretly hoping Brittany would stop worrying about her father.

o   o   o

Across the river, at a nearby restaurant, Billy Todd and his family were finishing their dinner.

"Hey, look. Did you see that light under the bridge over there?" Billy pressed his face against the window that overlooked the Fox River, cupping his hands around his eyes, to get a better look.

"It's probably just someone fishing," Mrs. Todd answered, as she studied the bill for their meal. She searched her purse for her wallet and was alarmed when she couldn't find it. "You know, Billy, I think that my wallet must have fallen out of my purse in the car. I'm sure that I had it when we left home. Would you go and check for me, please?"

"Sure mom. I'll be right back." Billy hurried outside. Because the restaurant's lot was full, their tan Impala was parked in the nature trail parking lot, right along the riverbank. As he reached the car, he saw the light under the bridge again. (The river was very narrow by this dam.) Even though it was on the other side of the river, he was sure he recognized the face. There was a woman trying to wipe something out of a little girl's eye. She held the light right in the girl's face.

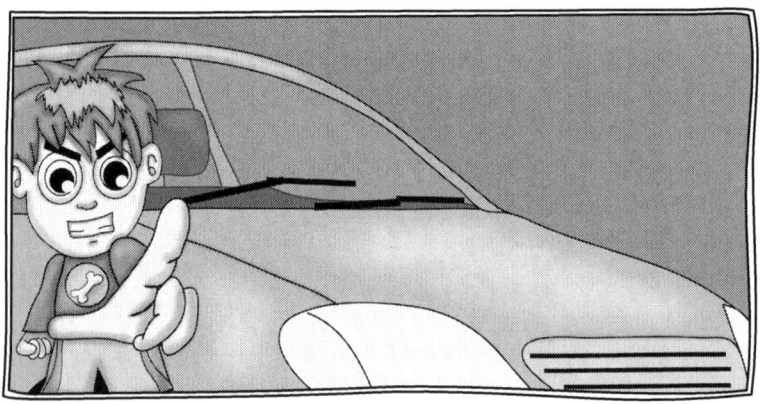

"Well, what do you know about that?" Billy said to himself. "It's the crybaby herself, little Miss Brittany. Gee, I can hardly wait to get to school on Monday to find out what she was doing out here, at this hour, with her blankets." He chuckled to himself, as he returned to the restaurant with his mom's wallet. "This will certainly make an interesting conversation at school during project time." He was still grinning when he reached his family's table.

"Oh, thank you, Billy." Mrs. Todd put the waitress' tip on the table, got up, and went to pay the bill as Billy and his older brother, Carson, followed. Carson was seventeen and had his driver's license complete with his own car. He didn't mind hanging out with his younger brother. Carson liked that Billy looked up to him. Billy was still chuckling to himself as they walked out the restaurant door.

"What's so funny, son?" Mrs. Todd asked.

"Oh, nothing, mom. I just thought that I saw someone I know from school." He grinned happily all the way to the car.

"Oh, I see the light now, Billy. It looks like some people are down there with blankets. Huh, I wonder what they're doing? Well, come on, boys; let's get in the car and go home. I'm tired." Sandra Todd got behind the steering wheel and drove out of the parking lot. As they crossed the bridge, Billy tried to see Brittany and whoever was with her but couldn't see anything—the light was out.

When they got home, Billy thought of a plan.

"Carson, I need your help."

"My help—what for?" Carson put on his lounging pants and headed for his computer.

"Do you remember that light that we saw at the river?" Billy sat down on the foot of his brother's bed. "I want to go back there and check it out. I thought that I saw someone I know down there."

"By the river, a friend of yours? It's kind of late for one of your friends to be down by the river, isn't it?" he said, turning on his computer.

"That's just it. I'm worried about him. I just want to see if he needs help." Billy lied. "So will you take me there?"

"What would mom say?" Carson looked away from the computer, right at his younger brother. "What's this really about?"

"You wouldn't help me if I told you. Just trust me, please."

"You've been acting weird ever since dad got called back into active duty. What's going on with you?"

"Nothing!" Billy stood up, irritated. "Are you going to take me or not?"

"Okay, okay. Simmer down." Carson motioned for Billy to sit back down. "We better keep this between us. I'm sure that mom wouldn't like us going out this late."

"The doctor has mom taking a sleeping pill since dad's been gone. If we wait for a little while, she won't hear a thing," Billy said and walked toward the door. "I'll wait for you downstairs. Mom said I could stay up and watch TV, since it's Friday night."

"I'll see you downstairs in about an hour. This better not be a wild goose chase."

"I'll owe you one for this, bro. Thanks a lot."

o o o

Brittany worked on her homework until she was just too tired to do anymore. "I'll finish the rest tomorrow, mom. Thanks for holding the flashlight. I don't know what I'd do without you." She packed up her book bag and snuggled down into the blankets. "Mom, we need to finish our conversation. Please tell me everything that you know about dad. Where is he?" She scrunched her pillow up under her head.

"Oh, Brittany, I have put off telling you because I have been waiting for more news about your dad. About three months ago, I got a letter that your father...Honey, your father's plane was shot down somewhere over Iraq," Victoria said, crying. She pulled her daughter close. "Brittany, I'm sorry, but I just got a letter at our post office box yesterday that daddy is still missing. They found his plane, but there was no sign of any of the crew, including your father. They are still searching for them, sweetheart." She tried to be brave for her daughter, but it was no use; the tears flowed uncontrollably.

"Mom...do you mean that daddy's dead?" Brittany joined her mother's agony and cried—harder than ever.

"No, Brittany, they don't know that he is dead only that he is missing."

As they continued to talk, Brittany calmed down. When Brittany felt the strength to speak again, she looked at her mother through teary eyes and asked, "Do you believe that he is dead, mom?"

"No, Brittany, I don't. I would feel it in my heart if he were dead. I believe that he is alive somewhere." She hugged her daughter tighter. "We must pray for him. Pray that God will take care of him. God knows where your daddy is. He will take care of him for us.

We'll have to be strong and carry on here until we know what has happened to him. Can we do that?" she said, drying her eyes with the blanket.

"Yes, mom...I'll try," Brittany said, finding the courage to smile.

"I miss your daddy terribly, but he would want us to be brave like him. I know that God will help us through this trouble, dear. We will be all right soon." She snuggled her daughter as they tried to go to sleep. "I love you, sweetie; goodnight."

"I love you too. Goodnight, mom." Brittany looked up into the stars and whispered, "Goodnight, daddy, wherever you are. I love you. I pray that we'll be seeing you soon." Brittany prayed as if her life depended on it—until she finally fell asleep.

CHAPTER 4
Spies

Carson's green jeep slowly crept out of the driveway and into the dark streets. He kept the headlights off until he was well down the street—they couldn't be seen by their mother.

"Man, Billy, your friend really better need our help. We're risking getting grounded you know," Carson said, turning the lights on as he rounded the corner.

"Don't worry. I just want to check it out—now lay off me!" Billy pulled his black hoody over his head and readied a flashlight from the big pocket in his pants.

"Touch-y-y-y! Say, what's buggin' you, for real? You're scaring me." Carson reached over and put his hand on Billy's shoulder.

"I don't want to talk about it, okay? Just drive. I want to go back to that bridge where I saw the light."

"Okay, okay, excuse me for caring. You're going to have to do my share of the dishes for the next two weeks for this favor." He jerked his hand off his brother's shoulder and put it back on the steering wheel.

"I'm sorry, Carson. I'm just mad. I'm mad about dad being gone; I'm mad about this stupid war; I'm just mad about a lot of things right now." He slumped down into the seat and crossed his arms angrily over his chest.

"I know that things are bad right now, little brother, but we have to be strong for mom. She doesn't need any more trouble. Just hang tight, okay? Dad will be back soon. I can feel it."

"Look, there's the bridge. Let's park over there and walk down under the bridge. I don't want anyone to hear us." Billy got out of the jeep and quietly closed the door.

"So what are we looking for?" Carson whispered, as he caught up with Billy, who was already crossing the street.

"I'll know it when I see it. Just follow me."

"You're pretty brave for a ten-year-old." The two boys crossed the road and went down under the bridge, where they saw the lights earlier. Much to their surprise, when they got to the riverbank under the bridge, they found blankets spread on the ground. Under the covers were two people sound asleep. Billy pointed his flashlight in their faces, but they didn't wake up.

"Oh my gosh—it's a woman and a little girl!" Carson couldn't believe his eyes.

"Come on—let's get out of here. Hurry up before they wake up!" Billy turned to run up the riverbank when suddenly he tripped over a rock and fell. "Ouch!" he yelled as he rolled back down and smashed right into the sound asleep Brittany.

Startled, Brittany and her mom woke up and screamed in fright. Victoria had to shake Brittany to get her to stop. Mrs. Dodson stood up and yelled at Billy, "Who are you? What do you want?" She took out the can of mace she had in her pocket and aimed it at the boys.

"We don't want anything, ma'am," Carson answered as he helped Billy up. "He just fell down. We're leaving. Sorry that we scared you. Come on, Billy."

"Billy Todd? Is that you?" Brittany looked right at her classmate. "What are you doing here? Oh, gosh, please don't tell anyone that you saw me sleeping here. Please, Billy, please."

Carson looked at his brother. "You go to school with this girl, Billy?"

"Yeah, and I see that she's a crybaby even when she's not at school." He picked up his flashlight. As he walked away, he said, "See you at school on Monday, crybaby."

Carson followed Billy to the jeep. "That's what you wanted—to be mean to a little girl?" Carson shook his head. "I can't believe that you made me help you to be mean to her. That'll be a month of dishes, or I tell mom."

"Alright, a month of dishes it is. I can't help it— that girl just annoys me." Billy put his hoody back in place and stared out the window as Carson drove the jeep.

"You're unbelievable; you know that? What would dad say?"

"Don't talk about dad. What does he care, anyway? He left us!"

"What? You're wrong if you think dad doesn't care. That's why he left, Billy— because he does care. Don't you understand that?"

"I said...I don't want to talk about it! Just be quiet!"

"Okay, have it your way, but you're wrong, Billy, real wrong." They were silent for the rest of the ride home.

o o o

Brittany and her mother were so shaken up by their intruders that they couldn't get back to sleep.

"Mom, this is terrible. What if he tells my whole class about us?" Brittany panicked, afraid of what Billy might say.

"Surely he wouldn't do that."

"You don't know him, mom. He's just a big bully and what's worse...he hates me." She trembled with fear. "Why else would he come down here and spy on us like that? How could he have found out?"

"That's a good question, sweetie. It really doesn't matter how... If he does tell everyone at school, we'll just have to deal with it. I'm so sorry about our situation, dear. If I get that job next week, we'll have a place to live in no time. I wish I had some relatives near who could help us, but there is no one. We have to rely on each other."

"We have God too. Don't forget him," Brittany said. "We need to ask God to help us too."

"I do every day, sweetie... every day. Let's try to go back to sleep. It'll be morning before you know it. Goodnight Brittany, and try not to worry."

"Goodnight, mom. I'll try, but that Billy Todd—he gives me a lot of reasons to worry." Brittany pulled the covers over her head and tried to think of better things.

CHAPTER 5
Community Search

The community center was active with Saturday-morning classes ranging from swimming to karate to jazzercise. It offered something for all types and ages of people. Brittany was the first to arrive, so no one could see her walk up with her mother. Victoria visited the nearby library while Brittany met with her schoolmates.

"Hi, Brittany," Maddison and DeVontay called, as they got out of their family's car. They could see that Alex, Brianna, and Caitlin rode together when Caitlin's mom dropped them off. Nehemiah rode up next, on the back of his grandfather's motorcycle.

"I'll call you when we're finished, Grandpa," Nehemiah said. His grandfather nodded in agreement.

"Welcome, gang!" Maddison pointed to the picnic table in front of the center. "Let's go over there and talk."

"I thought that we could just look around the city and see if we can see anyone who looks homeless," Alex suggested as she sat down. "If we do find someone, we can learn what they need and see if they would like some help. What if they have children?"

"Excuse me, Alex, but just what does a homeless person look like?" Brianna asked.

"I saw one on TV once—an old lady dressed in rags and pushing a shopping cart," Nehemiah added as he took a banana out of his pocket. "Sorry, I didn't have time for breakfast."

"I guess we could go look in the alleys or parks and see if there are any asleep," Caitlin suggested as she sat down next to Maddison.

"This is the Chicago *suburbs*." Caitlin took a drink from her water bottle. "Do you *really* think that there are homeless people here?" She rolled her eyes and crossed her arms.

"You know, guys...a homeless person doesn't have to look pathetic," Brittany said, taking off her sweatshirt and tying it around her waist. "They could just look like you...or me."

"You think so? Brianna raised her eyebrows curiously. "How will we ever find one then?"

"We'll know one when we see one," DeVontay said. "Why don't we divide into two groups? Maddison, Nehemiah, Alex, and Caitlin can go south. Brianna, Brittany, and I will go north."

"You guys have a cell phone?" Maddison asked, showing her phone to DeVontay's group.

"Maddison, you know that I have one," DeVontay said, waving his phone in the air.

"Okay, if you find someone, call me. I'll do the same on my end. If we don't find anyone, we'll meet back here in an hour, okay?"

"Sounds good to me," Nehemiah said as he got up from the table.

"Me too," Maddison said.

"Let's go," Brittany said, wanting to get this over. "If we don't find anyone, we'll see you in an hour."

"Wait. Let's set alarms for one hour." Nehemiah looked at his phone. "I've got 12:15 p.m."

"Unless we find a homeless person, we'll meet back here no later than 1:15 p.m." Maddison looked at the time on her cell phone. "See you later."

The kids split up into their groups and ventured out. No one really knew how to identify a homeless person, but they were confident in knowing when they saw one.

o o o

The two groups searched the city streets carefully but couldn't find anyone who looked homeless.

"I just think that we can't recognize anyone who looks homeless," Brianna said, adjusting her pink hat.

"We better get back to the community center. It's almost 1:15." DeVontay turned around and led the way back.

Just as they walked around the corner, Brittany spotted her worst nightmare—Billy Todd and a couple of kids from his group at school.

"Well, well, well... What have we here? It looks like the crybaby and a couple of her friends." Billy's face lit up with excitement.

"Lay off her, Billy," DeVontay spoke up. "Why do you keep bullying her anyway? What did she ever do to you?"

"Don't you know that no one likes a bully?" Brianna courageously stepped in, on behalf of her new friend.

All Brittany could do was look at Billy, with pleading eyes, shaking her head in desperation.

"You wouldn't stick up for her if you knew the truth," Billy bragged and walked past the group, bumping into Brittany as he passed. "See you in school on Monday, Brittany. I can't wait."

Brittany's group kept walking.

"What did he mean by that, Brittany?" DeVontay asked, looking puzzled.

"I...I don't know." Brittany watched Billy until he was out of sight.

"He's just pure meanness," Brianna added. "I don't understand kids like that. What makes a bully a *bully?*"

"Some people are just born that way," Brittany said as she looked at her watch. "Hey, it's getting late. Maybe you should call Maddison."

"It will be okay. I can see the center now." DeVontay pointed down the street. "By the way, Brittany, I disagree. I don't think that people are born bullies. I think that something happened to make them lose faith in people—something is bothering Billy. We used to be good friends at one time. He's not the same person I used to know. I need to try and find out what's wrong, but first, this project."

"There's the rest of the group waiting for us." Brianna said, running up to Maddison. I hope you guys had better luck than we did. We couldn't find anyone who looked homeless."

"We couldn't either," Nehemiah said. "Maybe Mr. Navarro can give us some ideas."

"Did anyone look up organizations that help homeless people?" Maddison asked, showing Brianna her new purple hat—she really loved purple.

"It's adorable, Maddison." She traded hats with her for a moment.

"Girls! Stop it with the hats already," DeVontay said, trying to grab Maddison's hat. "Yes, I looked up some, but I found something else. It's not for homeless people, so maybe it'll be easier to research. This organization helps people who need to get out of their apartment, but really can't afford to buy a house."

"That sounds interesting and much easier," said Nehemiah. "We could interview some people who live in apartments."

"What's the name of that organization, DeVontay?" Alex asked as they sat back down at the picnic table they shared earlier.

"It's called Habitat for Humanity, and I'll be ready to tell you all about it in class on Monday." DeVontay was successful in grabbing Maddison's hat.

"Hey, give it back! You're just jealous because you can't fit a hat over those silly corn rolls of yours." Maddison giggled pulling her hat out from under him and putting it back on over her black hair.

"Did you say silly?" DeVontay tried to control his temper. "I'm going to forget you said that, Maddison. We have more important things to talk about. Look, there's mom, Maddison. Here comes your grandfather on his motorcycle too, Nehemiah. That is so awesome!" DeVontay and Maddison got in their car and drove away.

"Can we give you a lift somewhere, Brittany?" Caitlin asked before heading to her mom's car with the rest of the girls.

"No, thanks, I'm meeting my mother over at the library. She's been waiting for me. Thanks anyway." Brittany scurried off.

"That girl is a mystery," Brianna said, shaking her head. "She's nice, but I can't figure her out. I don't get it."

CHAPTER 6
Billy's Bulletin

Mr. Navarro cheerfully greeted his students at the door as they entered his classroom Monday morning. The whole class was excited about their projects and that today was a half-day of school. As Brittany walked into the room, her eyes met Billy's. She looked away and didn't notice his foot sticking out in the aisle. Down she fell, hitting the floor hard. Her books flew out of her bag and scattered across the floor.

"Billy, why did you do that?" DeVontay was very tired of Billy's behavior toward Brittany. He stood at Billy's desk, continuing to badger him. "Why did you trip Brittany?"

"I just figured that if she liked to sleep on the ground, maybe she'd like to sit on the floor during class." Billy laughed at Brittany. "You little crybaby... Why don't you tell everyone where you slept Friday night."

"Billy, that will be enough out of you! I told you I have zero tolerance for bullying in this classroom. Go to the principal's office, and stay there for the rest of the day!" Mr. Navarro escorted Billy to the door.

Before he left, Billy turned to the class. "I just thought that Brittany would like the class to know that she slept under a bridge with her mother last Friday night. Isn't that right, Brittany?"

"To the office *now, Billy!*" demanded Mr. Navarro. He said sternly, "I mean now Billy." As Billy left the room, he smiled back at Brittany. Horror-struck, she picked up her books, bumped Billy out of the way and rushed outside the room.

"Wait, Brittany, wait a minute. Please don't go," Mr. Navarro pleaded, but it was no use. She was already half-way down the hall.

"I'll catch her, Mr. Navarro." DeVontay dashed out the door after her. Down the hall, he raced until he caught up with her. "Stop, Brittany, please, stop. I just want to talk to you."

Brittany couldn't run anymore and dropped to her knees, feeling vulnerable. By that time, Mr. Navarro caught up to them. Out of breath, he stammered, "Brittany, are you all right? Please talk to me and tell me what's wrong. I only want to help you." He knelt beside her, pulled her chin up, so she could look him in the eyes. "Please don't be afraid. Talk to me. I can help."

Brittany broke down and finally told DeVontay and Mr. Navarro everything—how her mom lost her job and her father was now MIA in the Air Force Reserves. Everything had happened so fast. She didn't know what they were going to do.

"I don't know what to say, Brittany." DeVontay looked at the ground, feeling horrible guilt for any complaint he had made. "Why didn't you tell us on Saturday?"

"I was too embarrassed. We used to have an apartment and a car. Mom sold our car for money to keep our apartment. It wasn't enough, and now we've lost both. You don't realize how quickly everything can change. What were we supposed to do? We didn't have anywhere to sleep! We had no choice but to stay under the bridge to keep us out of the rain. It all happened so fast...so fast," Brittany said, whimpering. "It feels so good to finally tell someone."

"Now that you have told us, we want to help you." Mr. Navarro smiled and gave her a hug. "Come on—let's go back to class. Everything will be alright, I promise."

"Let me carry your books for you, Brittany." DeVontay said, grabbing her bag. Together, they headed back to the classroom. "You and your mom are not alone anymore."

CHAPTER 7
Habititus Fever

Back in the classroom, Mr. Navarro quieted the students and asked for a person from each group to present their project. Though they were eager to go first, DeVontay's group went last.

"Mr. Navarro, our group searched the streets on Saturday, looking to help a homeless person. We thought we would recognize one if we saw them on the street. It was Brittany who told us, but we didn't really hear her, that they could look just like you or me. They don't have to look like that pathetic person you might see on a TV show. Mostly they are just going through a hard time and they need our help. Brittany is that person—she's no different than us."

DeVontay grabbed his research notes about Habitat for Humanity. "I want to share what our group chose for this project. As you've just heard from other groups, there are several organizations that help the homeless. I'm going to tell you about an organization that helps people buy their own home when the bank won't loan them money because their income is too low. It's called Habitat for Humanity. A man named Millard Fuller, who was born in eastern Alabama, started it. He was born poor and his mother died when he was three. His father, who was a very religious man, raised him alone. To make a long story short, when Millard grew up, he worked hard and became a millionaire before he was thirty. He found out the hard way that money couldn't buy happiness when he almost lost his own wife and family while working so hard to make that money. Millard decided to get rid of all his money. Even though his friends tried to talk him out of it, he began selling his family's belongings, donating it to Christian nonprofits and educational funds. They decided to live out their faith by working for God. He wanted to help people build affordable homes. Mr. Fuller started Habitat for Humanity—with lots of help from volunteers and businesses all have a heart to help others, it won't be long until Habitat for Humanity will build a million homes around the world using Mr. Fuller's idea. This is not the complete story but just a quick summary. If anyone wants to research Habitat for Humanity International they can go on line at www.hfhi.org. I should also tell you that they have local Habitat for Humanity locations all over the world called affiliates. So we need to find the one closest to us and work with them if we want to help Brittany."

Maddison, Brianna, Nehemiah, and Caitlin joined DeVontay at the front of the class. Maddison spoke up, "One thing that people who want to have one of these homes has to do is help with the actual building of other people's houses before they can work on building their own house. They call it 'sweat equity' and it can be as much as 500 hours. That's where we want your help. Brittany and her mother need a home. Now we know they lost their apartment and they have a dream to live in their own home. I think we should all help so we can help make their dream come true. Are you with me?"

DeVontay continued. "I am not ashamed to admit I have caught the fever. It's called Habititus. We want it to infect you, too. If you want to catch Habititus Fever, stand with us!"

The whole class stood and cheered.

"You guys are wonderful!" Brittany joined her new friends at the front of the class and gave each one a hug. "Thank you for caring." This time, she cried tears of joy.

"This is a great idea for a project, and I declare Brittany's group the winner," Mr. Navarro said, standing with Brittany and her friends. "Catching Habititus Fever is a good thing and I hope everyone catches it. First, I think you better do a little more research to find out how they apply to be chosen for a house and how someone your age will be able to help so Habitat for Humanity can build their home. I want everyone to get involved in this project, help Brittany and her mom, that is, if you want to pass my class. Also, this group wins the trip to the Cubs game!" Mr. Navarro applauded. "Great job, group!"

Brittany and the gang jumped up and down, screaming and clapping in excitement.

"Excuse me, Mr. Navarro, I just remembered my research. I believe you have to be sixteen to actually work on a Habitat home, but I think it would be a good idea for us to be there to serve the volunteers water or lemonade and sandwiches while the adults work," DeVontay said.

"Yeah, please don't forget the sandwiches," Nehemiah said.

"I like it, DeVontay—good thinking. Can anyone else think of other ways to help?" Mr. Navarro listed the students' ideas on the blackboard.

Alexandria jumped up. "I can try to get people to donate furniture for their house."

"That's another good idea," Nehemiah added. "My church has a food pantry. I can make sure their refrigerator is full."

"I go to your church, Nehemiah," Caitlin said, standing up. "I can ask my parents to get our whole congregation to come and help build their house. They like to do projects like that."

Mr. Navarro's list grew as everyone in the class thought of different ways to help. The excitement continued to grow and spread. Everyone wanted to help Brittany and wanted others to come help too.

In fact, the noise from their cheering and applause made the teacher across the hall come to see what was going on. Soon Habititus Fever continued to spread throughout the school. Everyone was so excited that they could not stop talking about it.

Mr. Navarro pulled Brittany aside. "I will call Habitat for Humanity for you and your mother, Brittany and get the ball rolling. We'll find out what we have to do to get you the home you've been dreaming of. In the meantime, I don't want you sleeping under any bridge. Tonight I'm putting you up in a hotel then we'll figure out what to do next, and dinner is on me. Let's wait out front for your mother, but first we need to stop in the office and find out why Billy has been acting so mean lately."

Brittany hugged Mr. Navarro tightly then joined her friends in celebration.

"By the way, class is dismissed. See you tomorrow. Everyone did a great job on their projects," Mr. Navarro added.

CHAPTER 8
The Heart of a Bully

Brittany accompanied Mr. Navarro to the office, where she sat across from Billy. With a mean smirk on his face, he looked at Brittany while she just stared at the floor, trying to ignore him. Glancing out the office window, Mr. Navarro noticed Carson waiting in his jeep for his little brother. He went out to meet with him. While outside, he also ran into Victoria, who was sitting on the school steps, awaiting Brittany to be done with class.

"We have Billy Todd and Brittany in the office," Mr. Navarro said to Victoria and Carson. "I would also like to talk to both of you. Won't you please join us?"

"Billy Todd... Isn't he the boy who doesn't like my Brittany?" She looked worried. "What's wrong—is Brittany all right?"

"Yes, she's fine." Mr. Navarro helped Victoria to her feet. "I'll explain everything when we get inside."

"I can only imagine what Billy's been up to. He's been acting really weird since our dad's Air Force Reserve unit got called into active duty," Carson said, following them into the school.

"What did you say?" Mr. Navarro stopped outside of the office door. "Did you say your father was called to active duty?"

"Yes, Billy's taking it real hard. In fact, he told me the other night that he is real angry with our dad. Billy thinks he left because he didn't care about us." Carson shoved his hands in his pockets and lowered his head. "I don't know how to convince him that dad went to war not only because he had to but *because* he loves us and doesn't want the terrorists to come here."

"Can you get a hold of your mother? I really would like to talk to her about this." Mr. Navarro and Brittany's mom went into the office while Carson called his mother.

As he stepped into the office, Carson said, "I got in touch with her at work. She'll be here in about five or ten minutes." Carson put his phone in his pocket, glared at Billy, then sat in the chair next to him.

"Great, Carson. Thanks a lot. I think that we all need to talk." Mr. Navarro grabbed a folding chair and put it in the middle of the room. "Billy I'm going to start with you. Why don't you like Brittany? What has she done to deserve such horrible treatment?"

"She cries and whines so much...it annoys me." Billy looked at Mr. Navarro then down at the floor.

"I'm sorry that I annoy you, Billy. I've just been so upset lately..." Brittany looked right at Billy, determined to hold back her tears.

"Billy, was that you and your brother who scared us under the bridge Friday night?" Mrs. Dodson asked as she went to hug Brittany. "None of this is Brittany's fault, you know. I had just told her that her father's plane was shot down over Iraq. He's been missing for weeks, and we don't know whether he is dead or alive. We were sleeping under the bridge because my landlord evicted us from our apartment. After losing my job, I could not make the rent payments anymore. Even though I get money from the Air Force, it's not enough to pay our expenses, and we have lost everything. Billy, don't you think Brittany has a good reason to be crying all the time?" Victoria had her arm around Brittany.

Billy couldn't look at them. The feeling of guilt created a knot in his stomach. "Billy, don't you have anything to say to these ladies?" Carson pointed at them. "You owe them an apology. I'm sorry you tricked me into taking you there."

"Billy, I told you that this school has a zero tolerance for bullying. Unfortunately, the principal might want to suspend you," Mr. Navarro said sternly. "Especially if you can't even bring yourself to apologize for your behavior."

At that moment, the office door opened and Mrs. Todd came into the room. Following behind her was Mr. Todd in full uniform. "Dad!" Billy and Carson shouted and jumped up from their seats.

"Now there's a wonderful family reunion," Mr. Navarro said, smiling.

Brittany noticed Billy crying. "Who's crying now, Billy?" she asked, smiling. "You know...it is okay to cry sometimes." She gave her mom a big hug. "We're going to be okay, mom. My friends and Mr. Navarro have a plan."

Brittany's mom looked at Mr. Navarro. "The credit goes to Brittany's group and their project research. They found a wonderful organization called Habitat for Humanity—they build houses for people just like you. We are going to call them in just a little while and find out how you can be included in their housing program," he explained. "In the meantime—"

"In the meantime, Mrs. Dodson, let me introduce myself. I am Squadron Leader Joseph Todd, Billy's father, but I am also your husband's commanding officer. I am so sorry for what you and your daughter have been going through these past weeks.

However, I have news I'm sure will make you very happy." Mr. Todd stepped out into the hall and came back pushing a wheel chair, where Brittany's dad sat. "I believe this pilot belongs to you. We found him a couple of weeks ago, injured without his dog tags. He has recovered enough to come home. I needed to see my sons so I thought that I would personally deliver him to you."

Brittany and her mother couldn't believe their eyes. It was the answer to their prayers.

"Daddy!" Brittany cried as she raced to hug her father. Victoria rushed over to her husband in disbelief that he was actually there in front of them.

"How is this possible?" She cried, looking at Mr. Todd.

"We're just happy we found him. He is going to need your help during his recovery. As you can see, he lost his left leg in the plane crash, but soon he can be fitted with an artificial one. He'll be back on his feet in no time. We're very proud to bring him home to you."

"We are forever grateful. Words cannot express our joy and relief. He means the world to us. God Bless you." Victoria cried then kissed her husband.

As they continued their reunion, Billy's dad turned to his son. "There is another reason I am here, Billy. Would you like to explain why you feel I don't care about you, son?" He looked Billy in the eyes and put his hand on his son's shoulder. "Don't you know you and your mother are the very reasons I get up every day and do what I do? I love my family and country so much that when I see people being mistreated, when there are terrorists in this world...I believe it is our duty to help those in need. We have to fight the bullies of this world. Any kind of bullying is wrong, so when I heard that my son is becoming a bully... Son, it hurts me more than anything I could imagine. I expect you to make me proud. I want you to be kind and help people when they need it. Tell Brittany you are sorry. Not only are you sorry, but you will be sharing a room with your brother. Brittany can have your room until their new home is built. Her parents will stay in our guest room. I think that will just about make up for any trouble you have caused this little girl and her mother, don't you?"

"Yes, sir. Gladly, dad." Billy turned to Brittany and her mother. "I really am sorry for my behavior. I now understand why you cried so much. Please forgive me. I am going to be one of the first people in line to help when they build your Habitat house." A huge grin formed on Billy's face. This time it was out of sincere happiness. "I think that I'm catching Habititus Fever and it feels really good."

"Mrs. Dodson, I just happen to be the human resources director for a corporation here in Aurora, and I would like you to come by my office tomorrow morning," Mrs. Todd said, looking at Victoria. "I think

I have the perfect job for you. It's an entry-level job and doesn't pay very well, but at least you'll be working again by tomorrow." She shook Victoria's hand and watched a smile grow on Victoria's face.

"I'm sure you will easily qualify for a Habitat home with your new job and the fact that your husband is home." Mr. Navarro looked like he could burst with happiness.

Brittany and her mother were speechless. Brittany thought for a moment then pointed to heaven. "I knew God would answer our prayers; that's how He loves us."

There was a knock on the office door. Maddison poked her head in. DeVontay, Alexandria, Brianna, Caitlin, and Nehemiah were standing with her.

"We just wanted to make sure that you guys were alright and to give you our research papers. It has all of the information about how to contact Habitat for Humanity. We also sent around a sign-up sheet and collected 200 names of students who have caught Habititus Fever."

Maddison handed the papers to Mr. Navarro, walked up to Brittany, and gave her a big hug. "Everything is going to be fine—you'll see."

"It is now. Look, both my father and Billy's have returned from Iraq! I've made a new friend, and my family's going to get the home we've been dreaming about." Brittany turned to Billy and smiled. He grabbed his father's hat and put it on.

"Mom and dad," Brittany took her parents' hands, "do you suppose I could get a dog...I mean when we get our new house?" She looked at her parents, batting her eyes.

"One thing at a time, Brittany. We'll think about it and discuss it later, I promise." Her parents exchanged glances, but Brittany's dad turned to her and winked his eye.

"Excuse me, but also in my research," DeVontay added, "I found the best cure for Habititus Fever is to help others be able to move into a decent and affordable home. After we are done helping Brittany and her parents, we want to continue to help others to get new homes too."

"That's wonderful, kids. Hmmm DeVontay, I think you might need to do a little more research." Mr. Navarro tapped his foot while glancing at DeVontay and Maddison.

"Research what? What do you mean?" DeVontay was extremely puzzled.

"I think we may have to postpone that Cubs game trip." Mr. Navarro laughed. "You need to research how long it's going to take you and Maddison to get over the chicken pox. It looks like a bad case is breaking out all over both your faces!"

All the kids screamed when they looked at the twins and ran wildly out of the school. Mr. Navarro and the other adults couldn't help but laugh.

THE END

DISCUSSION QUESTIONS FOR HABITITUS FEVER

It is our intention that students will not only read the book, but will also have time to discuss these questions. Ideally, it would be great to have a parent or grandparent read the book with their own children or grandchildren and to talk about the book together. Discussions can also happen in a group settings such as a school, church or small group. Dialogue can be very healthy in developing one's opinions about a variety of everyday problems that students and their friends encounter.

These questions are intended to be conversation starters about a variety of topics. You do not need to use every question and may select the ones you like the most. Hopefully, each student will come away feeling empowered and encouraged that they can make a positive difference in the world and that their problems can be solved in a healthy way.

PRE-READING SURVEY:

Please check if <u>you</u> know <u>anyone</u> who has experienced any of the following:

☐ Having only one parent

☐ Becoming Homeless

☐ Not having friends at school

☐ A student struggling in school

☐ Going to a food pantry to get food

☐ Other people being mean to you

☐ A parent loses their job

☐ Someone that does not know you, helps you just because you need it

☐ Having to move away from your friends

☐ Having a family member get hurt badly or die

☐ Having a family member in the military

☐ Worrying about problems in your life

☐ People telling your secrets to others

☐ Friends defending you when others are mean to you

☐ Your family gets involved to make life better for someone else

CHAPTER 1: THE PROJECT

1.1 Thunder struck nearby and scared Brittany. What scares you?

1.2 Brittany's mom, Victoria Dodson, lost her job. What happens when a parent loses their job?

1.3 Maddison loved hats and loved to dress up. What are your favorite things you like to do?

1.4 Mr. Navarro was an excellent teacher. What makes a teacher an excellent teacher?

1.5 Billy Todd was mean to Brittany. What does Brittany have to do to make it stop?

1.6 The class was given a project to work on together. When you are assigned to do a group project, what do you usually do in the group?

1.7 DeVontay tried to defend Brittany when Billy Todd was mean to her. What should you do when you see someone is being bullied?

1.8 Brittany had a hard time trying to concentrate on her schoolwork. What causes you to have this problem?

CHAPTER 2: MEETING AT MADDISON'S

2.1 Nehemiah said they might not be able to go on a vacation because of money. What are some other things that happen when there is not enough money?

2.2 DeVontay told the group about Habitat for Humanity. Where is the nearest Habitat for Humanity to you?

2.3 The teacher, Mr. Navarro, knows that students can make a difference in their community when they get involved. Name some ways students help where you live.

3.1 Brittany was trying to keep it a secret that she did not have a home to go to. Do you think you would have reacted that way? How do you think you would react?

3.2 Brittany's mom, Victoria Dodson kept saying everything would be okay. What is wrong with people taking the opposite approach and giving up when bad things happen to them?

3.3 Many churches are involved in a PADS program. What is it and who is it meant for? Do you think those children also go to school someplace?

3.4 Billy Todd saw Brittany under the bridge. He chose to tell everyone just to be mean and to embarrass Brittany. Why do you think some people are like that? What can we do to change them?

3.5 Brittany prayed harder than she had ever prayed in her life for her dad. Different religions around the world believe in praying. What are things you pray for?

CHAPTER 4: SPIES

4.1 Billy Todd got his brother Carson involved in driving him back to the bridge. How do you react when someone asks you to do something that you know is wrong?

4.2 Billy was very angry about his father being gone to war. He was afraid and he felt like his father did not love him. What could Billy have done so he would not be so unhappy?

4.3 Most of us have a bed to sleep on at night and a place we go home to after school. Can you imagine what Brittany and her mom are going through? What do you think would be the worst thing about it?

CHAPTER 5: COMMUNITY SEARCH

5.1 Maddison's group went out to find a homeless person to help. That turned out to be too hard to do. What are some ways students your age can help others?

5.2 Billy Todd was a bully to Brittany. Are there any bullies at your school? Why are adults sometimes necessary to solve problems with bullies?

CHAPTER 6: BILLY'S BULLETIN

6.1 Brittany was horror-struck when Billy told the class that she slept under the bridge with her mom. What do you see others do when they are embarrassed in front of their friends?

6.2 Mr. Navarro showed real concern for Brittany and really wanted to help her get through what she was feeling. Teachers and other adults often want to help. Give an example of how an adult has helped you or one of the students you know.

CHAPTER 7: HABITITUS FEVER

7.1 Millard Fuller grew up poor yet he became a millionaire. Why is it the things you do now will affect what your life will be like as an adult?

7.2 Millard Fuller gave away his money to help other people live a better life. Why did this make him happier than working hard to make even more money?

7.3 The Habitat for Humanity family has to put in up to 500 hours of sweat equity. How long will that take to complete if Brittany and her mom both work seven hours every Saturday?

7.4 What is Habititus Fever and why is it a good thing?

CHAPTER 8: THE HEART OF A BULLY

8.1 Billy and Brittany did not have their father living at home with them. Why is it so hard to live this way, even if it is temporary?

8.2 Brittany was crying a lot and Billy was being mean. Do adults ever cry or be mean to others?

8.3 Some people have a church that they attend. How could the church help the family and how could the church help Habitat for Humanity?

8.4 There is a saying that it is better to give a hand-up instead of a hand-out. What is the difference?

8.5 Brittany and her mom were evicted from their apartment when they could not pay their rent. What do people do when they lose their house or apartment because they cannot pay the mortgage or rent?

8.6 Why is it important for us to help each other?

8.7 Are there some problems that require the help of others?

8.8 What did you learn from reading this book and talking about it?

AUTHOR BIOS

Wanda Jones-Nelson was born in the Midwest, where she now resides with her husband, Danny. She worked with her husband as Sunday school teacher, AWANA leader, children and adult choir director, church pianist, and assisted her husband as youth director while their six boys grew up. Now she and her husband are serving the Lord in the ministry of the Christian Motorcyclist Association. She also enjoys teaching piano and caring for her newest grandson.

Ron Kelso is married to Kathy and they have two children. Ron graduated with an Associate degree in Business, Undergraduate in Teaching and his Masters in Administration. In teaching and now, he lives his life to help others. He has volunteered in numerous places such as a food pantry, youth group leader, clothing ministry, church camps, coaching sports, church boards, tutoring, several community outreach programs and Habitat for Humanity. After completing 33 years of teaching in Naperville, Illinois he retired to dedicate his time to his passion of Habitat for Humanity's mission of partnering with incredible under resourced families to build affordable housing.

We would like to invite you to email
Ron Kelso or Wanda Jones-Nelson at
Habititus@FoxValleyHabitat.org to share
what this book has meant to you.
Yes, the story must go on.
We hope you continue to read the rest
of the series as they are completed.

Made in the USA
San Bernardino, CA
03 August 2016